# Donald's Ice-Skating Adventure

A Level Pre-1 Early Reader

By Susan Ring

Illustrated by Loter, Inc.

DISNEP PRESS

New York

Lexile:

LSU ☐yes
SJB ☐yes
BL: 1.2
Pts: 0.5

DISNEY PRESS

First Edition
Library of Congress Cataloging-in-Publication Data on file
ISBN 978-1-4231-1830-5

Manufactured in Malaysia
For more Disney Press fun, visit www.disneybooks.com

Today is the Great Skate Festival.

It will be a fun day!

Donald has new .

ice skates

He wants to win the ①.

blue ribbon

Everyone is at Star Lake.

The skating begins.

Donald's friends cheer. Go, Donald, go!

Uh-oh, Donald! Look out for that !

tree

That was close!

Donald wants to win the .

Donald has new  blue ribbon, but he needs
ice skates
more than that.

Let's call Toodles!

What does Toodles have to help

Donald?

He has a , a , and a jar

mirror          pillow

of .

honey

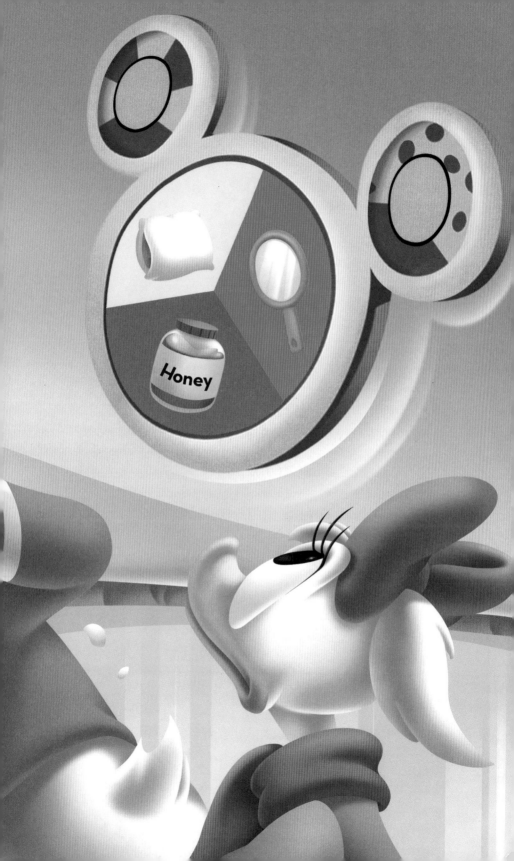

Donald is up again. Go, Donald, go!

His new  are fast.
ice skates

Oh, no! Donald is skating backward!

Mickey calls Toodles.

Mickey picks the .

He gives the  mirror to Donald.

mirror

Now Donald can see behind him.

Cheers! We've got ears!

Donald really wants to win the .
blue ribbon

He tries a fancy spin. Go, Donald, go!

But he spins and spins . . . and can't stop!

Oh, Toodles!

Minnie picks the  .

She pours some 🍯 on the ice.

It works! Donald's  stick to the

ice skates

.

honey

Donald slows down and stops. Hot dog!

Daisy has  for everyone!
hot chocolate

Donald loves .
hot chocolate

Oh, no! Donald is about to fall!

Oh, Toodles! Come quick!

Goofy picks the  .

He gives the  to Donald just

in time.

That didn't hurt a bit!

Donald gets his .
hot chocolate

But who will win the 🏅?
blue ribbon

Donald wins the !

blue ribbon

He did tricks that nobody else could do.

Hooray for Donald!